IDA HIKES IDAHO

by **Lori Otter** and **Karen Day**

in association with

Idaho Department of Parks and Recreation

Illustrated by **Chris Latter**

Copyright 2013 by Lori Otter. All rights reserved. ISBN 978-0-9885218-1-0, and ISBN 978-0-9885218-2-7. Published by I-Zing Books, Boise, Idaho. Printed in China.

Look for Tank's bone hidden on every park's page.

Welcome to *IDA HIKES IDAHO!*

I am so excited to share the beauty of Idaho with you. Our state parks are truly an amazing collection of all the best Mother Nature has to offer. Idaho's diverse and unique landscape is a gift that has shaped our history and will continue to sustain our future as long as we continue to steward nature's benefits. That's why our state park system is so important. For more than 100 years, our parks have insured the Gem State's outdoor treasures remain pristine for you and for generations to come. With boating, fishing, skiing, hiking, camping and tons of other options—our state parks have something for everyone, even our four-legged friends like Tank! And in return for all the parks offer us, we Idahoans must do just one thing: support our state parks!

How do we do that? First, remember that people like you and me have played a vital role in the creation and management of our park system. Forest rangers, firefighters, campers, hikers, boaters and mountain bikers—no matter how you and your family choose to enjoy our great Idaho outdoors—we all make a difference by visiting and caretaking our parks. Two simple ways you can help is to always clean up your campsite and to buy a Parks Passport that allows admittance to all 30 parks.

Our Idaho state park system is a blessing, offering us a wonderful way to experience nature's beauty while having lots of fun. Many families have had the opportunity to create precious memories because of time spent in our parks. Ida, Tank and I hope this book will inspire you and many more families to develop a lifelong relationship with nature while creating great memories in our state parks.

So grab a Parks Passport and come along with Ida and Tank to discover all the breathtaking sights and outdoor fun waiting for you in Idaho's state parks. You won't be disappointed! Ida, Tank and I guarantee it! Happy trails exploring Idaho's parks!

Esto Perpetua,

Tank

Lori J. Otter
First Lady of Idaho

IDA

Here is a map of Idaho's State Parks

 ATV/Motorbike

 Biking

 Boating

 Cabins

 Camping

 Climbing

 Disc Golf

 Fishing

 Group Events

 Hiking

 History

 Horseback Riding

 Learning

 Nordic

 RVs

 Snowmobiling

 Volunteering

 Yurts

 Family Friendly Trail

Idaho State Parks has a new icon with Ida's picture on it for "Family Friendly Trails."

ASHTON to TETONIA TRAIL

Welcome to Idaho's newest State Park!

I rode my bike 29 miles and hardly noticed I was going uphill because the view of the Teton Mountains made me forget! The trail is an old railroad bed with some spectacular trestles. I told Tank, "Don't look down!"

Esto perpetua, your friend,
Ida

The recommended direction to ride is from Ashton to keep the Tetons in view.

The trail is in good condition for biking and hiking, but keep in mind there is an 800-foot rise in elevation.

Many bridges and three trestles make for an exciting ride!

BEAR LAKE

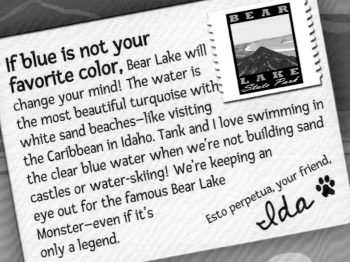

If blue is not your favorite color, Bear Lake will change your mind! The water is the most beautiful turquoise with white sand beaches—like visiting the Caribbean in Idaho. Tank and I love swimming in the clear blue water when we're not building sand castles or water-skiing! We're keeping an eye out for the famous Bear Lake Monster—even if it's only a legend.

Esto perpetua, your friend,

Ida

- Half of 20-mile-long Bear Lake is in Idaho and the other half is in Utah.

- The park has 60 campsites within 966 park acres filled with fishing, swimming and boating fun.

- Explorer and trapper, Donald MacKenzie, first named Bear Lake, Black Bears Lake, in 1817. Guess why?!

BRUNEAU DUNES

Stars, stars and more stars!

Far from city lights and filled with giant sand dunes, I see why this park is called "Idaho's Sahara." Last night Tank and I visited the observatory for some incredible galactic sightseeing. Today we went swimming in the middle of the desert! This park allows horses, so tonight I saddled up Cooper and galloped across the sand like an Arabian princess.

Esto perpetua, your friend,
Ida

- A shallow lake offers fishing and swimming with desert, prairie and dune habitats providing plenty of hiking, stargazing and wildlife observation.

- Oregon Trail pioneers mentioned the dunes in their diaries.

- The park has 4,800 acres with 98 campsites and two cabins for rent.

- Visitors can see the largest single-structured sand dune in North America at a height of 470 feet.

CASTLE ROCKS

Pinnacles, monoliths and outcroppings; those are some BIG words for some BIG rocks at Castle Rocks. Tank and I have been climbing up and down all day, and the views from the top just keep getting better. We spotted mule deer and a big-horn sheep with our binoculars. Tonight we're staying in a real bunkhouse. Next time I'll bring my horse Cooper because there's equine-friendly camping here.

Esto perpetua, your friend,
Ida 🐾

- Castle Rocks is only a few miles from City of Rocks State Park.

- An estimated 130 bird species live here! The park has 1,440 acres for hiking, mountain biking, climbing, photography and wildlife viewing.

- Discoveries of ancient Indian pictographs and stone tools indicate one of the oldest human cultures in Idaho inhabited this site.

7

CITY OF ROCKS
NATIONAL RESERVE

- City of Rocks is one of the finest granite-faced climbing sites in America with unique formations like Elephant's Head Rock, Monkey's Head and Twin Sisters.

- This 14,407-acre park is nestled in the Albion Mountains and is designated a National Historic Landmark.

- Wagon ruts from the Oregon and California Trail pioneers are still visible in this unique geological area.

Belay On!

That's what climbers yell when they are roped up and ready to go. Imagine climbing rock towers 60 stories high and that's City of Rocks! This park looks like a city built with boulders. Oregon Trail pioneers passed through here and wrote their names in axle grease. Today, Tank and I saw their emigrant signatures and 16 rare cliff chipmunks. Don't forget your helmet and ropes!

Estu perpetua, your friend,
Ida

COEUR D'ALENE PARKWAY

Tank and I have decided the best way to see the North Shore of Lake Coeur d'Alene is to glide or hike the Coeur d'Alene Parkway. We raced past sailboats on the lake and rolled smoothly by hikers, bikes, and people in wheelchairs. An ice cream cone and a swim is the perfect way to end a perfect day!

Esto perpetua, your friend,

Ida

- This park's paved trail connects with the North Idaho Centennial Trail, which runs 52 miles to Spokane, Washington.

- 1,000 feet of public shoreline along the 24-mile path offers picnic facilities, boat camping and beautiful lake views.

- Some of Idaho's best bald eagle viewing happens here from November to January.

COEUR D'ALENE'S
OLD MISSION

Today we visited the oldest building in Idaho!

The Old Mission was built by Jesuit missionaries and Coeur d'Alene Indians in 1850. The adobe church is like a time machine. Stepping inside you can see the 150-year-old handprints of the Indian builders in the dried mud walls!

Esto perpetua, your friend,
Ida 🐾

The Old Mission building was constructed of hand-hewn logs and without one nail!

You can still attend Easter Sunday Services and special events at the Mission.

The view from the Mission overlooks the ancestral homelands for many of today's Coeur d'Alene tribe.

The site is also known as Cataldo Mission, named for Father Joseph Cataldo, overseer in the 1880s.

DWORSHAK

- Ocean Spray Trail is an easy ¾-mile hike with great lake views. The trail is only available to visitors renting Three Meadows Group Campsite.

- The park is filled with family-friendly activities like volleyball, archery and horseshoes. The group site is completely private with cabins, meeting room, group kitchen and dining hall.

- A fish-cleaning station is near the boat dock to help with the day's fresh catch.

Did you know Dworshak Dam is the third tallest dam in the United States? The reservoir behind the dam is 19,000 acres of water fun! Tank and I are bringing the entire family back here next year to stay at three Meadows Group Campsite. We'll call it Ida's Private Summer Camp! Tank will bring the marshmallows.

Esto perpetua, your friend,

Ida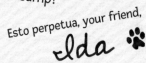

DWORSHAK STATE PARK

EAGLE ISLAND

- This 545-acre day-use State Park is ten miles northwest of Boise city limits.

- The Boise River borders the park on the north and south offering a great swimming beach.

- Future building plans include a golf course, camping and an ice skating rink!

Eagle Island is 15 minutes from downtown Boise featuring disc golf, horseback riding, hiking, canoeing, swimming and a waterslide. It's like having an awesome State Park in your own backyard! Tank especially enjoyed playing with his dog pal, Duke. Tank and I are already sharpening our skates for the future outdoor ice skating rink.

Esto perpetua, your friend,

Ida ✿

12

FARRAGUT

Farragut—what a fun surprise!

The 4,000-acre park is only 30 miles from Coeur d'Alene on Lake Pend Oreille, the biggest and deepest lake in Idaho! Tank and I swam, boated and learned all about submarines at The Naval Training Center Museum. The best part was the model airplane flyers field—up, up and away!

Esto perpetua, your friend,

Ida

FARRAGUT STATE PARK

- After the Pearl Harbor attack, the U.S. Navy built the second largest inland Naval Submarine Training Center where the park is now located.

- "Pend Oreille" means earring in French. The lake is named after the Kalispell Indians who lived around the lake and wore ear pendants.

- All forms of model aircraft can be seen flying at the RC field— fixed wing, rotary wind and unpowered soaring aircraft.

13

GLADE CREEK

Tank and I feel like Lewis and Clark!

The Corps of Discovery camped here at Glade Creek in 1805. You can read about this place in William Clark's journal. It's exciting to think we're following their footsteps! Maybe the explorers caught a few trout and cooked them for dinner—just like we did! We reeled in a tasty rainbow and cutthroat today!

Esto perpetua, your friend,

Ida

- You can learn about and see where Lewis and Clark camped through the Interpretive sign.

- The U.S. Forest Service manages 4 campsites off site. Situated on a river bend, the park offers a large private beach and is accessible to rafters.

- "...we fell on a Small Creek from the left which Passed through open glades." Captain William Clark, September 13, 1805.

HARRIMAN

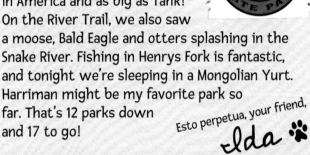

Have you ever seen a trumpeter swan?

They're the biggest waterfowl in America and as big as Tank! On the River Trail, we also saw a moose, Bald Eagle and otters splashing in the Snake River. Fishing in Henrys Fork is fantastic, and tonight we're sleeping in a Mongolian Yurt. Harriman might be my favorite park so far. That's 12 parks down and 17 to go!

Esto perpetua, your friend,

Ida 🐾

Railroad baron, Averell Harriman, and family donated this former 11,000-acre cattle ranch to Idaho in 1977. It's often called the "Railroad Ranch."

This park lies within a 16,000-acre wildlife refuge. Twenty-two miles of trails are open year round.

The Cattle Foreman's House, Ranch Manager's house and the Bunkhouse are available for group rentals.

HELLS GATE

- Hells Gate State Park is the gateway to Hells Canyon and Idaho's Lewis and Clark country.

- The Lewis and Clark Discovery Center offers informative exhibits and a film "From Mountains to the Sea," a documentary on the journey of the Corps of Discovery.

- The interesting Nez Perce National Historic Park is only 30 minutes away.

- The First Day Hike Loop Trail is a family-friendly 1.3- or 2.5-mile hike that offers glimpses of wildlife and provides access to the beach, river and playground.

Ready for a rip-roaring ride? You're invited on our next rafting trip through Hells Canyon! To stay dry, you can take a jet boat instead, but slow down to see petroglyphs. As for Tank and I, we love WHITEWATER. To keep your feet on the ground, try Trapper's Trail. Look for beaver, otter, deer, fox, and if you're lucky—bighorn sheep!

Esto perpetua, your friend,

Ida

HENRYS LAKE

- The three-mile Aspen Loop Nature Trail is family-friendly and handicap-accessible.

- The area has been inhabited for 10,000 years. Shoshone, Bannock, Blackfeet, Crow, Flathead, Nez Perce and Sheepeater tribes fished, hunted and gathered bulbs here.

- Yellowstone, Grand Teton National Park, Red Rock Lakes National Wildlife Refuge, Mesa Falls Scenic Byway and Harriman State Park are all close to Henrys Lake.

This is no fish tale!

Tank and I hauled in a 12 lb. trout today! Henrys Lake is world-famous for HUGE fish and that means we're going eat a HUGE dinner. Wish you were here. The fire is crackling, the fish is frying, and the stars are HUGE and bright and reflecting in the lake—it's like we're camping in heaven!

Esto perpetua, your friend,

Ida

HEYBURN

Captain Ida

Welcome to the oldest park in the Pacific Northwest and the first state park in Idaho! Heyburn is over 100 years old, but it still looks beautiful, especially cruising on Chatcolet Lake. With three lakes, this park is half water, so don't forget your swimsuit and captain's hat. Ahoy mate!

HEYBURN STATE PARK

Esto perpetua, your friend,
Ida

- The park is named after Senator Weldon B. Heyburn for his pioneering efforts to establish park lands.

- Before Heyburn became a park, Coeur d'Alene Indians gathered here for hundreds of years.

- In early years, the famous steamboat IDAHO carried many park visitors from Coeur d'Alene to the park.

LAKE CASCADE

Tank and I were on our way to McCall . . .

but got sidetracked at Lake Cascade. Fishing, swimming, boating, waterskiing, windsurfing—we just couldn't pass up 41 square miles of water fun just an hour north of Boise! We'll be back this winter to hit the slopes at Tamarack and try some cross-country skiing on the trails around the reservoir.

Esto perpetua, your friend,

Ilda

The park offers 246 campsites next to Lake Cascade with 86 miles of shoreline.

- Crown Point Trail is 2.6 easy miles and groomed for year-round use.

- Cascade is the only park that offers three rentable group yurts with lakeshore views.

LAKE WALCOTT

- Warblers, eagles, hawks, pelicans, owls and tundra swans offer the best bird-watching in southern Idaho.

- Lakeshore amenities include 41 campsites, two cabins, six picnic shelters, acres of shady lawns and a playground system.

- Bluegill, pumpkinseed, green sunfish, smallmouth bass and rainbow trout—Lake Walcott is like a fish zoo, except you can catch them!

Walcott is in the middle of the Minidoka National Wildlife Refuge, and the bird-watching is fantastic. Bring your binoculars! Better yet—have you ever played disc golf? The park has a free, 18-hole disc golf course where you try to throw discs into baskets. Tank beat me—TWICE!"

Esto perpetua, your friend,
Ilda

LAKE WALCOTT
STATE PARK

20

LAND OF THE
YANKEE FORK

At the Interpretive Center in Challis, you can see museum exhibits, historic photos and try gold panning.

The historic Challis Bison Jump site is available for viewing on Highway 93.

Bayhorse, Bonanza, Custer and Yankee Fork are famous mining ghost towns in the area.

Bring your gold pan!

Tank and I are trying to strike it rich in this historic mining area. We visited ghost towns called Bonanza and Bayhorse but didn't see any ghosts. We did see a real gold dredge and learned that gold and silver played a big role in Idaho's history.

Esto perpetua, your friend,
Ida 🐾

LAND OF THE YANKEE FORK
STATE PARK

21

LUCKY PEAK

I can't believe we're windsurfing 8 miles east of Boise! No wonder Lucky Peak is one of the most popular parks in Idaho. Beaches, marinas, boat ramps and endless trails open year-round for hiking, mountain biking, cross-country skiing. Hike a mile and you'll find five backcountry yurts for rent—so much solitude so close to home!

Esto perpetua, your friend,

Ilda

Sandy Point is a 34-acre recreation area with a giant fountain, beach volleyball and swimming. Brave souls take a frigid Polar Bear Plunge here every New Year's Day.

The scenic Boise greenbelt runs all the way from Eagle to Lucky Peak State Park.

The Discovery unit of the park is so named after the William Price Hunt party that discovered the Boise River and its "Treasure" valley.

MASSACRE ROCKS

If you want to touch history,
come to the "Gate of Death." That's what Oregon Trail pioneers called this narrow rock passage that only allowed one wagon to pass through at a time. Ten pioneers died by Indian attack here in 1862. Tank and I watched an amazing sunrise over the Snake River—but Massacre Rocks was not always so peaceful.

Esto perpetua, your friend,
Ida

MASSACRE ROCKS *State Park*

- Wagon wheel ruts and emigrant names from the Oregon Trail can still be seen within walking distance of the Interpretive Center.

- Evidence of past volcanic history is visible in the geologic rock formations.

- Muledeer, coyote, muskrat, beaver and over 200 species of birds have been sighted in the 900-acre park.

McCROSKEY

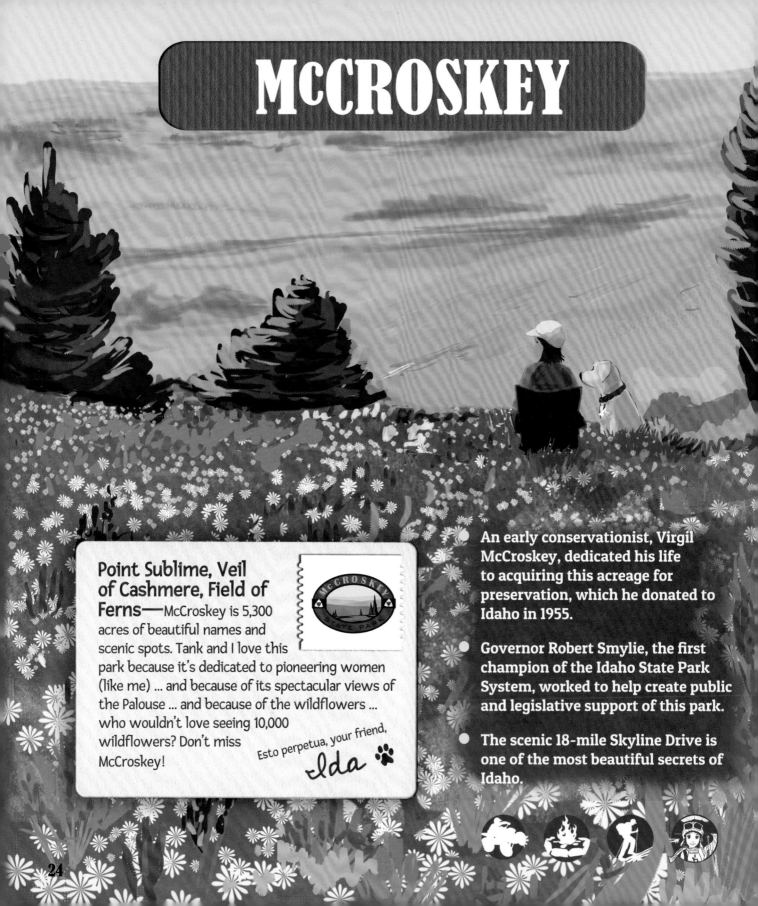

Point Sublime, Veil of Cashmere, Field of Ferns—

McCroskey is 5,300 acres of beautiful names and scenic spots. Tank and I love this park because it's dedicated to pioneering women (like me) ... and because of its spectacular views of the Palouse ... and because of the wildflowers ... who wouldn't love seeing 10,000 wildflowers? Don't miss McCroskey!

Esto perpetua, your friend,
Ida

MCCROSKEY STATE PARK

- An early conservationist, Virgil McCroskey, dedicated his life to acquiring this acreage for preservation, which he donated to Idaho in 1955.

- Governor Robert Smylie, the first champion of the Idaho State Park System, worked to help create public and legislative support of this park.

- The scenic 18-mile Skyline Drive is one of the most beautiful secrets of Idaho.

MESA FALLS

- Mesa Falls is not a State Park, but viewing areas are operated by Harriman State Park staff jointly with Targhee National Forest.

- These are the last unfettered falls on the Columbia River System.

- A new road and the historic Big Falls Inn, with museum and visitor center, provide easy and informative access.

I'm trying to imagine 1901, back when John Henry Hendricks and his family were homesteading here at Upper and Lower Mesa Falls. I bet these waterfalls were spraying rainbows in the air just like today. Next time we see a park ranger, I'm going to thank him for preserving these rainbows!

Esto perpetua, your friend,

Ida 🐾

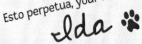

PONDEROSA

Ponderosa State Park

is filled with four seasons of fun. Tank and I can't wait to come back next summer to swim and water ski on Payette Lake. On the cross-country ski trail we saw a fox, a bald eagle and the tallest ponderosa tree in Idaho—150 feet and still growing! All this only two hours north of Boise— Amazingly Idaho.

Esto perpetua, your friend,

Ida

- The history of this park started in 1905 when citizens lobbied the Legislature to preserve the famous giant ponderosa pines.

- Visitors can enjoy 1,515 beautiful acres with 163 campsites and modern cabins and group sites for rent on the lake front.

- Possibilities for outdoor activities are endless with camping, hiking, cycling, kayaking, canoeing, mountain biking, volleyball, horseshoes, swimming, fishing, snowshoeing, cross-country skiing, and wildlife/wildflower viewing.

PRIEST LAKE

Tank and I have been picking huckleberries all day. Our buckets are empty, but our tummies are full! Priest Lake has two lakes: upper and lower—so we're having two-times the fun on the water! This lake is so clear it's like floating on blue glass in the middle of the Selkirk Mountains. There's nothing better than Idaho huckleberry ice cream!

Esto perpetua, your friend,

Ida 🐾

- The State Park, open year-round, has 151 campsites and lies just 30 miles from the Canadian border in Idaho's lush, green panhandle.

- 2,400 feet above sea level, the lake is 19 miles long and 300 feet deep with a placid, two-mile passage between lakes.

- Nell Shipman, an early silent film pioneer, produced the movie, "The Grub Stake," near Lionhead campground. Guided walks and an interpretive center provide film history for campers.

HUCKLEBERRY FESTIVAL

27

ROUND LAKE

How many kinds of trees can you fit in Idaho's Panhandle?

So far, Tank and I have seen red cedar, western hemlock, ponderosa pine, white pine, western larch and Douglas fir and that's just around our campsite at Round Lake. This park is a wild and peaceful place, except for the bullfrogs. They're singing non-stop for their supper. I wonder if frogs like marshmallows ...?

Esto perpetua, your friend,

Ida

- The first 40 acres of Round Lake State Park were purchased for $5,000 in 1955.

- Near Sandpoint, the 58-acre lake was formed in the Pleistocene Epoch by glacial activity.

- The park remains beautifully primitive and campsites only accommodate tents and small RVs.

THOUSAND SPRINGS

- Malad Gorge is 250 feet deep and 2.5 miles long and visible from I-84, but Devils Washbowl is just out of sight from the interstate.

- Oregon Trail emigrant journals often mention the lovely Thousand Springs area.

- Vardis Fisher, a famous Idaho author, wrote most of his 38 novels at Billingsley Creek.

Tank and I have found

five beautiful reasons to visit the Magic Valley: Malad Gorge, Billingsley Creek, Niagara and Crystal Springs and Earl M. Hardy Box Canyon Springs Nature Preserve. This park is 110 acres of scenic spots to hike and picnic with waterfalls, hot springs and a Devil's Washbowl! You can also see the Hagerman Horse close by. These fossils are 3.5 million years old!

Esto perpetua, your friend,
Ida

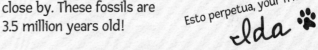

TANK

THREE ISLAND CROSSING

- Three Island Crossing State Park is located near I-84 and Glenns Ferry, a town named after Gus Glenn, who built a ferry across the Snake River in 1869.

- Situated in the high desert, the park campground is a surprise oasis of grass and shade trees near the river.

- Read original Oregon Trail journal entries about the dangerous crossing and watch the re-enactment of pioneer crossings the second Saturday in August.

What was it like to travel in a covered wagon? Bumpy, dusty, hot and DANGEROUS, especially when the Oregon Trail crossed the roaring Snake River without a bridge! That's what Tank and I learned at this park's History and Education Center. Did you know some pioneer kids might have walked the entire 2,170 miles?

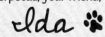

Esto perpetua, your friend,

Ida 🐾

TRAIL OF THE
COEUR D'ALENES

A former railroad grade through Idaho's silver country, the Trail was cleaned of mine tailings, paved and opened to the public in 2004.

Take the Sierra Silver Mine Tour and visit both Old Mission State Park and cross Chatcolet Drawbridge to enter Heyburn State Park along the path.

Learn the important history of railroads in Idaho at the Northern Pacific Railroad Historic Depot in Wallace.

73 miles of smooth asphalt with 17 scenic wayside stops, 36 bridges and HIGH trestles—that's the Trail of the Coeur d'Alenes from Plummer to Mullan. This scenic path is perfect for feet, paws and wheels (non-motorized). Along the way, Tank and I rode the world's longest gondola up Silver Mountain!

Esto perpetua, your friend,
Ida

TRAIL OF THE
COEUR D'ALENES

WINCHESTER LAKE

Winchester Lake is the only park in Idaho named after a city that is named after a rifle! But all you need is a fishing pole to enjoy this lake's tasty rainbow trout, even in winter. Tank and I are keeping warm and cozy, camping in a park yurt, while the snow flies. We saw a pack of real wolves at the Nez Perce Wolf Education and Research Center. Last night we heard them howling at the moon, and Tank joined in!

Esto perpetua, your friend,
Ida

This park is open year-round, with four yurts and 71 campsites.

A visitor center and guided tours of the 20-acre Nez Perce Wolf reserve is within walking distance of the lake.

Gasoline engines are not allowed, so bring your canoe and paddles!

IDA'S TOP 10
JUNIOR PARK RANGER TIPS

1. Drink plenty of water.
2. Wear proper clothing and footwear.
3. Keep bug spray and sunscreen handy.
4. Always wear your life jacket in and around water.
5. Make sure your adults know where you are.
6. Be campfire smart—make sure all fires are out before you leave.
7. Stay on the trails when hiking.
8. Keep a first aid kit nearby.
9. Be respectful of all park critters.
10. Make sure your campground is clean of any trash when you leave.

Idaho Animals Word Search

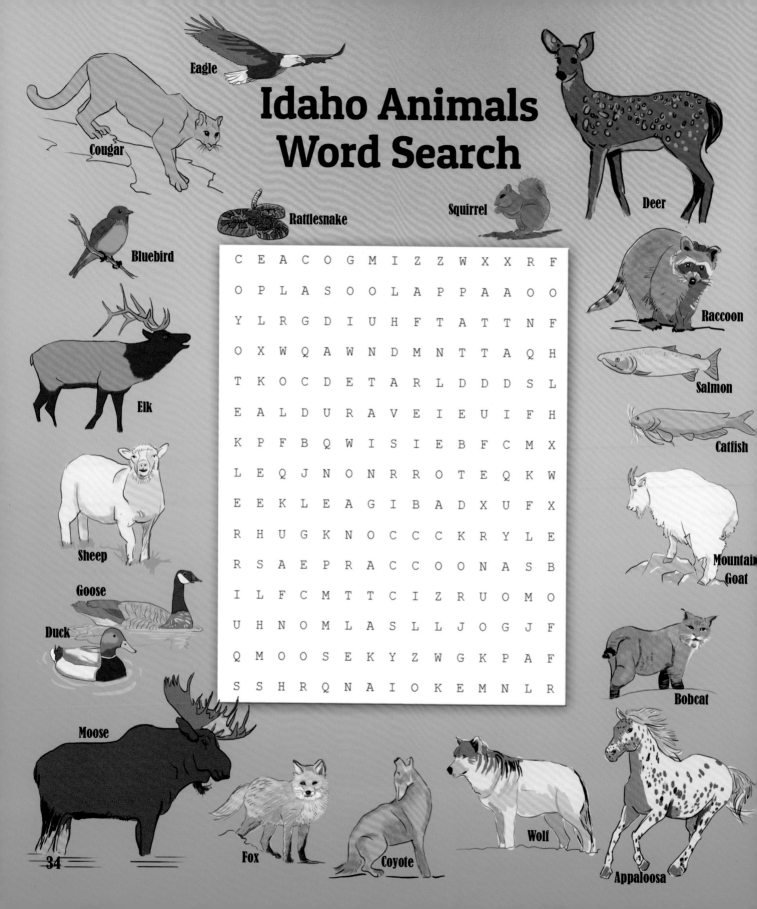

Eagle

Cougar

Deer

Rattlesnake

Squirrel

Bluebird

Raccoon

Salmon

Catfish

Elk

Sheep

Mountain Goat

Goose

Duck

Bobcat

Moose

Fox

Coyote

Wolf

Appaloosa

```
C E A C O G M I Z Z W X X R F
O P L A S O O L A P P A A O O
Y L R G D I U H F T A T T N F
O X W Q A W N D M N T T A Q H
T K O C D E T A R L D D D S L
E A L D U R A V E I E U I F H
K P F B Q W I S I E B F C M X
L E Q J N O N R R O T E Q K W
E E K L E A G I B A D X U F X
R H U G K N O C C C K R Y L E
R S A E P R A C C O O N A S B
I L F C M T T C I Z R U O M O
U H N O M L A S L L J O G J F
Q M O O S E K Y Z W G K P A F
S S H R Q N A I O K E M N L R
```

HELP TANK FIND HIS BONE

SPECIAL THANKS to Governor C.L. "Butch" Otter, the Idaho State Commerce and Tourism Department and the hardworking men and women of the Idaho Department of Parks and Recreation who keep these special places open and accessible for all to enjoy.

Many years ago, Senator Weldon B. Heyburn and Governor Robert E. Smylie began setting aside beautiful and historic places in Idaho, designating them as state parks, knowing these special lands would enrich the lives of future Idahoans.

Today, people have been enjoying state parks in Idaho for over a century, and you play an important role in making sure that these places remain beautiful and safe places to enjoy the outdoors.

There are so many things to see and do within Idaho's State Parks. Use your "Ida Hikes Idaho" book to collect commemorative stamps at each state park as you travel across Idaho. Become a Junior Ranger! Pick a park and let your adventure begin.

Visit us on Facebook and learn more about how to enjoy and support Idaho State Parks at **www.parksandrecreation.idaho.gov.**

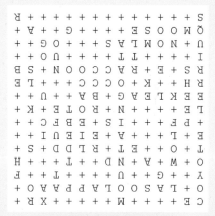

WORD SEARCH SOLUTION

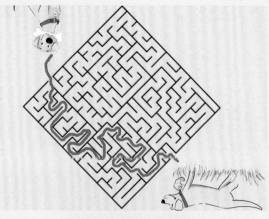

TANK'S MAZE SOLUTION